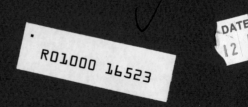

A Mitzvah
Is Something Special

By Phyllis Rose Eisenberg
Illustrated by Susan Jeschke

Harper & Row, Publishers
New York, Hagerstown, San Francisco, London

A Mitzvah Is Something Special
Text copyright © 1978 by Phyllis Rose Eisenberg
Illustrations copyright © 1978 by Susan Jeschke

Library of Congress Cataloging in Publication Data
Eisenberg, Phyllis Rose.
    A mitzvah is something special.

    SUMMARY: A young girl who hopes she will be able
to understand a mitzvah when it happens does
one for both of her grandmothers.
    [1. Grandmothers—Fiction] I. Jeschke, Susan.
II. Title.
PZ7.E3463Mi   [E]   77-25664
ISBN 0-06-021807-X
ISBN 0-06-021808-8 lib. bdg.

For my mother,
Frances Blossom,
and in memory of my mother-in-law,
Lena Eisenberg

Grandma Esther is my favorite grandma who likes to call me *Bubeleh* (that means little grandmother) even though my real name is Lisa.

Grandma Esther is my daddy's mother. She says I look just like Daddy did when he was my age, only he was a boy.

Grandma Esther always says, "Take care of your teeth, Bubeleh, so you'll be like me—not a false one in my head and only four fillings."

"Let me see them—let me see them," I say, because she always tells me good stories about her fillings. She opens her mouth wide and there are her four beautiful, solid-gold fillings. "When did you get this one?" I ask, pointing to one in the back.

"When I was going to marry your Grandpa Nathan, I was ashamed that he should have to pay for my dental work. So I saved from my paycheck for a whole year and had this filling done the day before our wedding."

"And what about this one?" I ask, pointing to a bumpy one on top.

"By then," says Grandma Esther, "your daddy was born. But I had no one to leave him with so I could go to the dentist. But when my neighbor, Anna Dubinsky, saw I had a toothache, she said, 'Esther, go. I'll take care of the baby.' So I did. And when I got back, she had already fed and diapered him. Then, Bubeleh, she made me hot tea. Oh, it was a real *mitzvah* and I'll never forget it."

"What is a *mitzvah*, Grandma?"

Grandma Esther puts her hands on my shoulders the way she does when she has something important to tell me. "A mitzvah, Lisa, is like a good deed, only much more." Then she looks into my eyes until I feel like some of Grandma Esther is right inside of me. "A mitzvah is a very big blessing. When Anna Dubinsky did what she did, to me *that* was a mitzvah."

Dorrie is my mama's mother. She says I look almost like Mama did when she was a little girl.

Dorrie is my favorite grandma who likes to call me food things like Cookie Pie. And that is really funny because she hardly ever cooks or bakes.

Dorrie wears tinted contacts and has two wigs— a short and a long.

At Dorrie's apartment, I put on her long wig and her green robe and her platform shoes. Then I use my pretend voice and say, "Good morning, I'm your neighbor, Mrs. Noodle Pudding."

"How nice to meet you, Mrs. Pudding," says Dorrie, using her pretend voice, too. "I was just having some gumdrop wine and merry berry pie. Will you join me?"

"No, thank you, Dorrie," I say. "I came here to do you a mitzvah."

"Say, Cookie Pie," says Dorrie, using her own voice, "how do you know about mitzvahs?"

I tell Dorrie about Grandma Esther and Anna Dubinsky. Then I say, "Did you ever have a neighbor like that who did you a mitzvah?"

"Well, Cookie Pie," she says, "when I was little, we knew a flute teacher. He was very poor so my mother and father gave him food and clothes. He wanted to do something nice, too, so he gave me free flute lessons."

"Were the lessons fun?"

"No, I had to practice every day for two whole years. Oh, how I hated it!"

"But Dorrie, how could that be a mitzvah?"

"I didn't know it was a mitzvah then, Lisa, but I know it now. Now I love to play the flute."

"But are mitzvahs only for grown-ups?"

"I don't know, Cookie Pie," says Dorrie, "I never thought about it."

"Dorrie, would you pour some gumdrop wine while I think about it?"

While I sip my wine and eat my merry berry pie, I keep wondering if I will know when a mitzvah happens to me. I hope I do.

Grandma Esther is a very good cook and baker and she is teaching me how to make strudel. So far I'm adding the nuts and raisins and preheating the oven to 350°. Someday she's going to let me roll the dough all by myself. When I learn how to make strudel all the way, I might teach Dorrie how to do it.

Grandma Esther is also very good at making quilts. Whenever I sleep over, I sleep in her bed and she always tucks me in with a beautiful quilt she made long ago.

"A bubeleh like you should go to sleep early," Grandma Esther always says, even though I tell her that at home I watch TV until I fall asleep. (It only happened once, but I keep forgetting to tell her that part.) "You've got to grow," she says.

"I'm always growing," I say. "Even when my eyes are open."

"I don't like you to be up so late. Good night, my Bubeleh," she says, and we give each other some big, squishy hugs.

Later, I turn on the light and count the quilt squares. So far I'm up to eight daisies, fourteen polka dots, nine roses and twelve stripes. If I ever take quilt lessons, I'll make one with a million squares so it will be big enough for Grandma and me when we're older and bigger.

Dorrie has a very long hair growing out of her chin that you can see only in bright light. When I say, "Dorrie, your chin hair grew again," she stops what she's doing and pulls it out. Then she says, "What would I do without you, Cookie Pie?"

Dorrie has lots of pictures on her walls and so many plants I think I'm in a pretty forest. Gus painted all the pictures and he grows the plants, too. Gus is Dorrie's friend.

At Dorrie's, I sleep on her living-room sofa, except when her friend Sandra is there. Then Dorrie calls me and says, "Sandra's sleeping over this weekend, Lisa. You'll have to come another time."

"How come, Dorrie?" I say. "How come Sandra gets to sleep over and not me?"

"She's very lonely, Cookie Pie. Her best friend moved away. So I'll try to cheer her up."

"When Sandra stays with you, are you doing a mitzvah?"

"I don't know, Cookie Pie," Dorrie says. "I just know that people are happier when they're not lonely.... Lisa, how about coming here *next* weekend—okay?"

"It's not so okay, Dorrie," I say. "I was planning to visit you *this* weekend. Why can't someone else cheer up Sandra?"

"Sandra needs me," says Dorrie. And then her voice gets wrinkly and she says, "I'm sorry to disappoint you, Cookie Pie. I really am."

When she says it like that, I know she understands my sadness. So I say, "Okay, Dorrie, see you next weekend." But I'm still not very happy.

I wonder if Sandra thinks it's a mitzvah that Dorrie is going to cheer her up? I would, because Dorrie is very good at cheering.

I hope that a mitzvah happens to me before I am very much older.

When I tell Grandma Esther about Dorrie's cheering Sandra, she says, "That reminds me of Grandpa Nathan. He cheered people, too." Then Grandma Esther nods the way she does when she thinks of Grandpa Nathan.

"What was he like?" I ask. She has already told me, but I like to hear it again.

"He was as good as gold. There wasn't a mean streak in his whole body. If only he could have lived to see my little Bubeleh," says Grandma Esther. "Lisa, do you know what I pray every night—every night so help me?"

"What, Grandma?"

"That I live long enough to dance at your wedding. And that you will have a good man like Nathan so you can have a good life."

"My daddy says that a good life means doing whatever means a lot to you. And that I should be thinking about that right now."

And Grandma Esther smiles and says, "Your daddy is a smart man and a good man. He's just like your Grandpa Nathan."

I tell Dorrie about my Grandpa Nathan, and she says, "Your Grandpa Al is just the opposite. He's loaded with mean streaks. It was good riddance when he left."

"Where did he go, Dorrie?"

"Who knows? Maybe he's on a mountaintop some-where, or living in a lemon tree or—"

"No one could live in a lemon tree," I say.

Dorrie puckers up her mouth until her crease disappears. "Grandpa Al is a lemon, Cookie Pie, so he'd be right at home." And she laughs so hard I think she will never stop. Finally she says, "Believe me, Lisa, I don't miss him."

"Would you miss Gus?"

"Yes," she says. "I like Gus."

I like Gus, too. Especially when he makes hot dogs on a hibachi out on Dorrie's balcony. And plays his guitar while Dorrie plays her flute. Gus sings songs that sometimes make me sad, but I like them anyhow. I even know the words to three of them.

I tell Dorrie, "I might be a folk singer when I grow up, or maybe an actress."

"Whatever you do," she says, "you'll always be my Cookie Pie."

"But, Dorrie, what if I grow up and become president of everything—you couldn't call me Cookie Pie then!"

"I'd call you President Cookie Pie."

"Would you bake strudel for me if I was president?"

"No, Lisa, I wouldn't."

"But, Dorrie, wouldn't you be proud of me if I was president of everything in the world?"

"I'll always be proud of you, Cookie Pie, but I'll never bake strudel. Period."

I guess that Dorrie will never do things she doesn't care about. But for things she likes, like gumdrop wine and music and cheering, there's no one like Dorrie.

And there's no one like Grandma Esther for strudel and quilts and weddings, because that is what she's good at.

For stories, Dorrie is the best in the world for the mean-streak kind. But for the gold-filling kind and the good-as-gold kind, no one is better than Grandma Esther.

I thought Dorrie and Grandma Esther cared about everything different, but they *both* care about me. So one night when my parents were going out...I invited them to sleep over.

Esther, your strudel is delicious," says Dorrie. "And your music makes me dance," says Grandma Esther.

"This seems like a mitzvah," I say. "Is it?" "It's such a big mitzvah, Lisa," Grandma Esther says . . . "That we'll remember it forever," says Dorrie.